For Caroline and Sumner
M.W.

For Kevin, Patrick and Alex
A.R.

First published 1996 by
Walker Books Ltd
87 Vauxhall Walk, London SE11 5HJ

This edition published 2001

2 4 6 8 10 9 7 5 3 1

Text © 1996 Martin Waddell
Illustrations © 1996 Arthur Robins

The right of Martin Waddell to be identified as author
of this work has been asserted by him in accordance
with the Copyright, Designs and Patents Act 1988.

This book has been typeset in Monotype Ellington.

Printed in Hong Kong

British Library Cataloguing in Publication Data
A catalogue record for this book is
available from the British Library.

ISBN 0-7445-7839-6

THIS WALKER BOOK BELONGS TO:

_____

_____

_____

_____

WHAT USE IS A MOOSE?

written by
Martin Waddell

illustrated by
Arthur Robins

WALKER BOOKS
AND SUBSIDIARIES
LONDON • BOSTON • SYDNEY

Jack made friends with a moose in the woods, so he brought the moose back to his house.

"What use is a moose?" asked Jack's mum.

"I'm sure mooses have uses," said Jack.

"If you find a use for your moose, he can stay," said Jack's mum.

Jack and his moose sat in the garden and thought.

"I could hang washing out on you, Moose," Jack suggested. So he hung washing out on the Moose. But…

That was no use!

"Can you drive, Moose?
You could be Mum's
chauffeur!" Jack said
to the moose. But…

That was no use!

"Maybe you could dig the garden!"
said Jack. But…

That was no use!

"Could you cook Mum her tea?" Jack asked the moose. But…

Even that was no use!

"Your moose is wrecking our house!"
Mum told Jack, and she got very cross.
"We've no use for a moose!" she said.
"He'll have to go back to the woods."

Jack was upset. So was the moose. "You must be some use," Jack told the moose.

So the moose did his best to help round the house.

"Oh, no!" said Mum.

"Not that way!" said Mum.

"No, no, no!" cried Mum.

"OH, *NOOOOOOO!*"

But it was too late...

CRACK

CRASH

CRUNCH

"You're a very bad moose!" said Mum, pulling Jack up from the floor.

The moose shivered and quivered and shook.

"Get out of my house!" Mum told the moose. "You're no use and I don't want you here any more!"

The moose went away.

Jack cried and cried for his moose.
"That moose was no use!" said his mum.
"But I *love* my moose," Jack told Mum.

Mum thought a bit, then she said,
"You're right, Jack. Being loved is a
very good use for a moose." And she
called the moose back.

The moose stayed with Jack almost for ever, but not in the house. It lived in a special moose shack out the back, built by Jack …

and the moose!

Martin Waddell's inspiration for **What Use is a Moose?** came while he was on holiday in the USA. "I dreamed up this story one morning in a small wood in Vermont," he says. "What use *is* a moose? I don't know, but there is something strange and sad about them."

Martin Waddell is one of the finest contemporary writers of books for young people. Twice winner of the Smarties Book Prize – for *Farmer Duck* and *Can't You Sleep, Little Bear?* – he also won the Kurt Maschler Award for *The Park in the Dark* and the Best Books for Babies Award for *Rosie's Babies*. Among his many other titles are *Amy Said*; *Who Do You Love?*; *Owl Babies*; *Night Night, Cuddly Bear* and *A Kitten Called Moonlight*. He was the Irish nominee for the 2000 Hans Christian Andersen Award. He lives with his wife Rosaleen in County Down, Northern Ireland.

Arthur Robins says, "Let's be serious, have you ever tried to draw a moose? Well I can tell you, it's no use: fidget, fidget, fidget. 'Have you finished drawing me yet?' 'No! Sit still and stop humming!' 'Can I have a look?' 'No, not yet.' 'I'm hungry. Can we go for tea and cakes?' 'Moose! That's a very good idea!' It's no use to draw a moose."

Arthur Robins has illustrated numerous books, including the Walker picture books *Mission Ziffoid*, *The Magic Bicycle*, *The Teeny Tiny Woman* and *Little Rabbit Foo Foo*. He is married with two daughters and lives in Cranleigh, Surrey.

ISBN 0-7445-6945-1 (pb)

ISBN 0-7445-7742-X (pb)

ISBN 0-7445-3651-0 (pb)